P9-EEU-567

CH

DEC - - 2000

ROAR!

A Noisy Counting Book

by Pamela Duncan Edwards   illustrated by Henry Cole

HarperCollins*Publishers*

For sweet Lizzie Lawley, who came
"roaring" into the world on October 26, 1998
With love,
P.D.E.

For Mom, who taught me my numbers,
my colors, and a whole lot more
With love,
H.C.

The artwork for this book was created using acrylic paints
and colored pencil on hot press Arches watercolor paper.
Roar!
Text copyright © 2000 by Pamela Duncan Edwards
Illustrations copyright © 2000 by Henry Cole
Printed in the U.S.A. All rights reserved.
http://www.harperchildrens.com

Library of Congress Cataloging-in-Publication Data
Edwards, Pamela Duncan.
  Roar! / by Pamela Duncan Edwards ; illustrated by Henry Cole.
    p.   cm.
  Summary: A lion cub's roar frightens away other colorful animals, from one red monkey
to eight brown gazelles, that he wants to come play with him—until he encounters nine
other lion cubs.
  ISBN 0-06-028384-X. — ISBN 0-06-028385-8 (lib. bdg.)
  [1. Lions—Fiction.   2. Jungle animals—Fiction.   3. Counting.   4. Stories in Rhyme.]
I. Cole, Henry, 1955-   ill.   II. Title.
PZ8.3.E283Ro   2000   99-34958
[E]—dc21   CIP

Typography by Elynn Cohen
1   2   3   4   5   6   7   8   9   10
❖
First Edition

One day, while great big lions lie basking in the sun,
A jolly little lion cub goes off to find some fun.

ROARS the little lion cub,

"Who will play with me?"

1 red monkey rushes up a tree.

Friendly little lion cub feels a little sad,
Plods down the pathway—pad, pad, pad.

He **ROARS** by the lake,
"Will you walk with me today?"

2 pink flamingos flap and fly away.

Puzzled little lion cub begins to feel upset.

"There must be others who want to play.

I just haven't met them yet."

He **ROARS** even louder,

"Would you like to join my game?"

3 orange warthogs cry,
"No, thank you, just the same."

Downhearted little lion cub sets off for his den.

But then he thinks that maybe he'd like to try again.

"Shall we dance?" **ROARS** the lion cub.

"Let's wiggle, bounce, and roll!"

4 blue lizards slither down a hole.

Unhappy little lion cub sniffs and starts to cry.

"Nobody will play with me, and I don't know why."

"Hello!" **ROARS** the lion cub.

"May I use your muddy slide?"

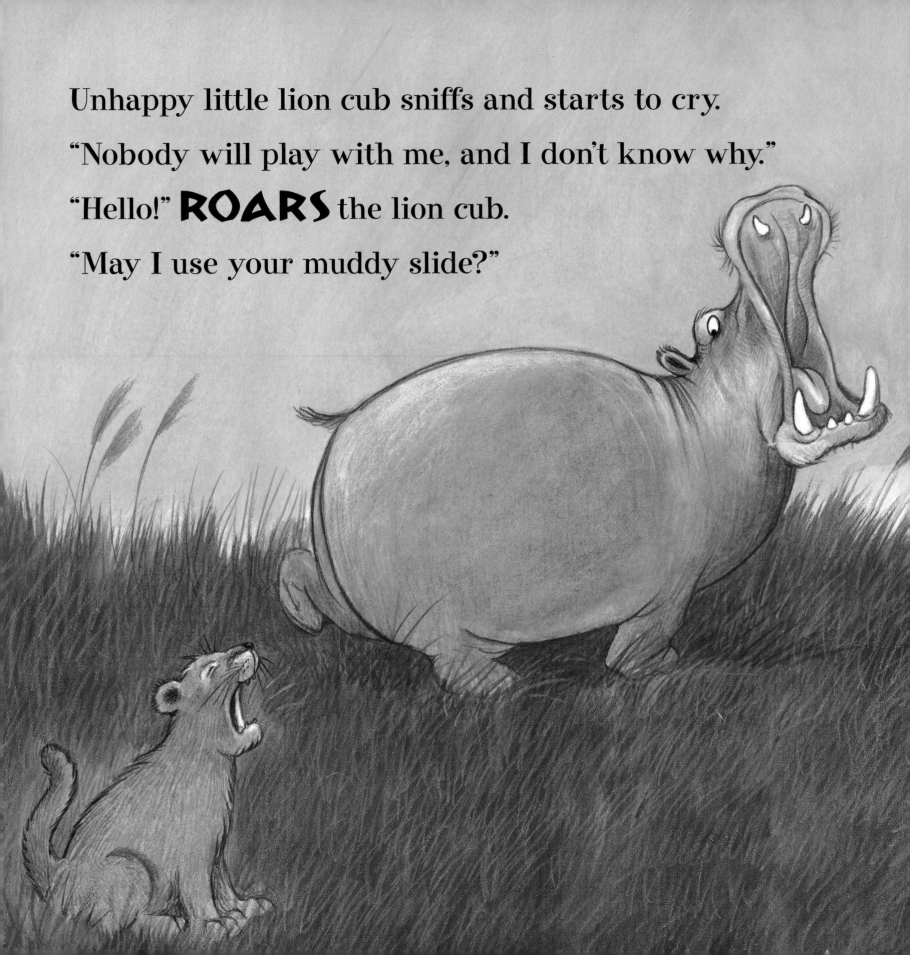

5 gray hippos shake their heads and hide.

Dismal little lion cub isn't very sure

Why everybody runs when they hear his playful **ROAR**.

"How about," **ROARS** the lion cub,

"swimming in the river?"

6 green crocodiles make the tall reeds quiver.

Gloomy little lion cub, whenever he draws near,

ROARING in his nicest voice makes everyone disappear.

He **ROARS** across the grassland,

"I'm not having any fun!"

7 black rhinos kick their heels and run.

Glum little lion cub, his loud and sudden **ROAR**,

Gives everyone a shock and makes their ears sore.

"Let's picnic," **ROARS** the lion cub.

"Shall we find food to eat?"

8 brown gazelles race off on pounding feet.

Lonely little lion cub still hasn't found a friend.

But suddenly he hears a noise coming around the bend.

"Wow!" **ROARS** the lion cub.

"Look at what I see!

9 yellow little lion cubs **ROARING**

just like me."

"Come with us," **ROAR** the lion cubs.

"Together we'll explore."

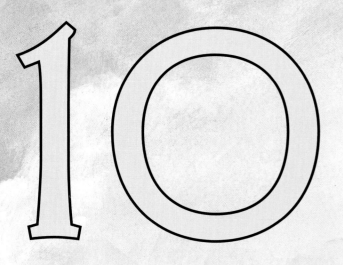 **10** happy little lion cubs